Aladdin

by Barbara Hayes

Brown Watson

ENGLAND

The Magician

Long ago and far away, there lived a boy named Aladdin. His father was dead and his poor mother could not prevent the boy from running wild around the streets.

One day a rich-looking stranger came to town. He stopped and spoke to Aladdin. He told him that he was his uncle, the brother of his father. "I have been away for forty years, but now I have come back to stay," smiled the stranger.

When Aladdin told the stranger that his father was dead, and that he and his mother were very poor,

the stranger seemed upset. "I am your uncle," he said. "I will provide you both with all you need." The stranger, though, was not Aladdin's uncle. He was a wicked magician.

Later, he and his servant brought gifts of food and clothes to Aladdin's home. Aladdin's mother was puzzled. She had never heard that Aladdin's father had had a brother! But, because they were poor, she took the gifts.

The magician went on giving Aladdin and his mother
money and presents. One day, he bought Aladdin a fine
pony, and took him riding far into the countryside.

"Would you like to be rich?" asked the magician, and
when Aladdin said "yes", he went on, "Then, if you do a
simple favour for me, you and I will always be rich."

Even though Aladdin felt nervous, he agreed because
he was sure it was better to be rich than poor!

They rode on into the mountains for several miles. At
last they stopped, and the wicked magician told Aladdin
to get down from his horse and build a big fire.

As the fire blazed up, the magician chanted magic words and threw powder into the flames. At once, thick coloured smoke swirled into the air, the ground shook, and a heavy stone trapdoor appeared.

The magician slipped a ring on to Aladdin's finger. "This ring will keep you safe," he said. "Now lift this stone. Go down the stairs beneath it and you will come into a lovely garden full of riches. They are yours. Help yourself to what you want." So Aladdin grasped the ring handle of the stone trapdoor.

To his surprise, Aladdin found he could lift the heavy
stone easily, but when he saw the dark stairs leading
downwards, he was afraid and wanted to go home. Then
his so-called uncle showed his true nature as a wicked
magician. He smacked Aladdin and forced him down
into the darkness. "Stupid boy! You can find yourself a
fortune," he growled. "All I ask for myself is that you
should bring back to me the old lamp that you'll find in
the garden."

Poor Aladdin had no choice but to go down the long
flight of stairs.

The Lamp

At the foot of the stairs, Aladdin found himself in a wonderful garden filled with fruit trees. But instead of fruit, the trees were laden with rubies and diamonds and emeralds. Aladdin picked as many as he could carry and tucked them into his clothes. He knew that his mother would be pleased with such fine gems and that they were worth a lot of money.

Then Aladdin looked round for the old lamp.

"I had better find it," he thought. "If I do not return with it, the man who says he is my uncle will be cruel to me again. He might not let me out through the trapdoor."

Aladdin walked slowly through the garden, and across a bridge over a stream. Finally, in a far dark corner, he saw a bright light burning.

"That must be the lamp," he thought with a sigh of relief.

Aladdin carried the lamp back through the garden.
When he reached the stairs, the magician screeched,
"Hand me the lamp!"
    "Let me out first," said Aladdin.

The magician was furious when he heard these words.
    "You have broken the spell, you stupid boy," he
shouted. "Since you will not give me the lamp willingly
while you are still in the cave, it can be of no use to me."
    He was so very angry that the magician slammed shut
the heavy stone trapdoor. Then, waving his hands, he
chanted an evil magic spell.
    "You will never open this door again," he yelled. "I am
the only person who knows where you are, Aladdin!
Now I am leaving for a distant country. Here you will
remain forever! While you live, you will regret not doing
as I asked!"
    Then the magician rode away.

Poor Aladdin tried and tried to push up the stone slab
and escape into the fresh air, but the trapdoor, which he
had lifted so easily a few minutes before, now stayed
firmly shut.

At last, when he was quite worn out, Aladdin crept
down the stairs and sat in a corner of the garden. He
was cold and hungry, but there was no fruit on the trees
for him to eat, only precious gems. The magic garden,
which had seemed so wonderful earlier, now held no
attractions for him.

He set the old lamp at his side, and clasping his hands
together he prayed that somehow he would soon see his
mother again. As he did so he chanced to rub the ring
which the magician had given to him. In all the
excitement, Aladdin had forgotten about it.

At once there was a flash of light, and in a cloud of smoke a huge genie appeared out of the ring. "I am the slave of the ring," he said in a deep voice. "Your wish is my command."

Aladdin was terrified at the sight of the huge figure, but he thought quickly and said, "Please take me home to my mother."

Instantly, he was gone from the magic garden, still clutching on tightly to the gems and the lamp.

In the very same instant, Aladdin found himself back in his own home, standing in front of his mother. The genie had gone, but he still had the gems in his clothes, and he also had the lamp.

Aladdin's mother was amazed to see her son safe at home, but very pleased, of course. She listened, astonished, as Aladdin told her all that had happened, explaining that the so-called uncle was really a magician from a distant land, who had only tried to become their friend in order to get his hands on the old magic lamp.

Puzzled, Aladdin's mother picked up the lamp. "I wonder why he went to so much trouble just to get this old thing?" she said, giving the lamp a rub with her sleeve. Suddenly, in a billowing cloud of smoke, another genie appeared.

"I am the genie of the lamp," he said. "Your wish is my command."

Aladdin was growing quite used to magic and was not so startled as before. Quickly, he said that they wanted a huge meal brought to them. The genie obeyed, and then disappeared back into the lamp.

Aladdin and his mother ate the food and then they noticed that it had been served on dishes and plates of the most expensive gold and silver.

Aladdin was able to sell the plates in the market and get enough money to keep him and his mother for the rest of their lives. The market traders were very surprised at the good fortune of Aladdin.

The Princess

"People might think we have stolen the plates," said Aladdin's mother. "Do not rub the lamp any more. Put it away."

So the years went by quite happily, until Aladdin became a man. Then one day, while out walking, he saw the king's daughter, Princess Badroul, and fell instantly in love with her. When Aladdin told his mother that he wanted to marry the princess, she was horrified.

"Only princes marry princesses. Not humble boys like you," she said. "The king will put you in prison for even thinking of it."

But Aladdin would not change his mind. He brought out the jewels he had taken from the underground garden so many years before, and told his mother to take them to the king as a gift. Although she thought it was a great mistake, his mother agreed to go.

With her knees trembling, Aladdin's mother bowed to the ground before the king. The jewels spilled from her shaking hands and rolled on to the floor.

"My son begs you to take these jewels as a gift and asks for the hand of your daughter in marriage," she whispered. The king's courtiers gasped in astonishment.

Everyone thought Aladdin and his mother would be flung into prison for daring to ask such a thing. But the king could see that the jewels were finer than any he had ever seen, and he was greedy for more.

"Tell your son he can marry my daughter if he gives me forty trays of fine jewels carried by forty strong servants. Then, if that is satisfactory, he must build a palace next to mine, equally magnificent, for my daughter to live in when she is married. And all this must be done in a day."

Aladdin's mother rushed home to tell him the news.

"You can never do all that," sobbed Aladdin's mother.

But Aladdin carefully wrote down all the king's requests, then he fetched the magic lamp from where it had been at the bottom of a trunk for years and years. He rubbed it hard. There was a roll of distant drums, a cloud of smoke, and the genie was in the room.

"I am the slave of the lamp. Your wish is my command," he said.

Aladdin gave him the king's list of orders.

The genie of the lamp had wondrous powers. He clapped his hands and forty servants carrying forty trays of fine jewels appeared in an instant. They were sent straight to the king.

Next, the genie and Aladdin stood before the royal palace. With another clap of his hands, the genie built a palace far finer than that of the king, and he filled it with lovely furniture and rich tapestries, the finest china, gold and silver dishes, engraved knives and forks, as well as a host of elegantly dressed servants.

The Magician Returns

When the king saw all these wonderful things, he decided Aladdin must be a very rich magician, and that made him the right person to marry the princess. The wedding took place at once, and the young couple were happy together for several years. But the magician, living far away, felt furious every time he reminded himself that he did not have the magic lamp.

One day, the magician heard about Aladdin and his riches and how he had built a palace in a day. The magician guessed at once that Aladdin must have escaped from the cavern and taken the magic lamp with him. The magician studied his books of spells to discover how to get the lamp for himself.

He disguised himself as a seller of lamps, and travelled to the magnificent palace, where Aladdin lived with the princess. He waited outside until he saw Aladdin leaving, giving money to poor people as he went. The magician was filled with jealousy.

Then the evil magician walked up and down, calling, "New lamps for old. New lamps for old." He gave a new lamp to everyone who brought him an old one. What a bargain! One of the servants thought of the old lamp she had seen at the bottom of one of Aladdin's chests. Not knowing that it was a magic lamp, she brought it out and gave it to the magician.

However, the magician knew it was the magic lamp. At once he threw away all the other lamps, new and old. He smiled a wicked smile and rubbed the lamp. The genie appeared and, of course, had to obey his new master.

"Take me, this palace, and everything in it to the desert of Morocco," ordered the magician.

At once, there was thunder and lightning and balls of fire in the sky, and the palace disappeared as if it had never been. When Aladdin rode back home, he found that nothing remained. The palace, the princess, the lamp and all his wealth were gone. Needless to say, the king was furious.

He commanded Aladdin to bring the princess and the palace back. When he could not, the king ordered Aladdin to be flung into prison. By good fortune, though, Aladdin was still wearing the magic ring which the magician had given him many years before.

He had forgotten all about its powers, because he had
been using the magic lamp. Suddenly he remembered.

The genie of the
ring was not as
powerful as the
genie of the lamp,
but he whisked
Aladdin to the
deserts of far-off
Morocco, where
his palace now
stood. There,
Aladdin heard the
wicked magician
telling the princess
that she must
marry him at once
because she would
never see Aladdin
again. Aladdin was

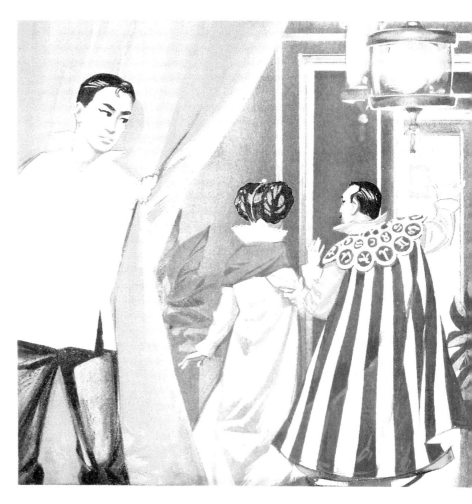

desperate. He spoke to a passing servant girl who
remembered her young master. She told him that the
magician kept the magic lamp always tucked into his belt.

Only the power of the lamp could give Aladdin back his
princess and his palace. He knew that he must get the
lamp. So, as the magician sat feasting with the princess
and his friends, Aladdin crept up behind him and put a
sleeping potion into his drink.

The magician
drank deeply. He
rubbed his eyes. He
sank lower into his
chair and at last he
fell asleep. Aladdin
stepped forward and
snatched the lamp
from the magician's
belt. The princess
jumped to her feet
with joy at the sight
of Aladdin.

The magician's
friends ran away into
the desert and back
to their own homes.

Then Aladdin rubbed the magic lamp. There was a roll of
distant drums and a flash of light. A cloud of smoke rushed
from the lamp, and with it came the genie. "I am the slave
of the lamp. Your wish is my command," he smiled,
bowing to Aladdin.

"Then transport
this palace and
everything in it back
to where it stood
before, beside the
king's palace,"
ordered Aladdin.
"After that, make the
magician disappear
forever so that he
will not trouble
anybody in this
kingdom again."

So all was as it had been before. The palace re-appeared next to the king's palace and Aladdin, his princess and his mother lived there for the rest of their happy lives.

As for the wicked magician, he vanished completely and was never heard of or seen again.

Aladdin forgave the king for putting him in prison. The magic lamp was put somewhere very safe where nobody but Aladdin could reach it. The magic ring he wore always, but he summoned the two genies only when there were happy occasions such as royal marriages, or when the kingdom was in danger.

First Published 1993

Published by Brown Watson, The Old Mill, 76 Fleckney Road
Kibworth Beauchamp, Leicestershire, England

© 1993 Martspress Ltd

ISBN 0-7097-0897-1

Printed in Belgium